Welcome to the clan, Helena Marion Long. Your Nana loves you!

Huge thanks to Victoria Rock and Sara Gillingham for helping to shape my vision of Thumbelina's story and to Kathy for suggesting it. Thanks to Antonia for being my Thumbelina model, Quinby for being the prince, mouse, and blue-eyed fish, and to Linda Belous, for being Thumbelina's mother.

Library of Congress Cataloging-in-Publication Data
Long, Sylvia.
Sylvia Long's Thumbelina.
p. cm.
Summary: A tiny girl no bigger than a thumb is stolen by a great ugly toad and subsequently has many adventures and makes many animal friends, before finding the perfect mate in a warm and beautiful southern land.
ISBN 978-0-8118-5522-8
[1. Fairy tales.] I. Andersen, H. C. (Hans Christian), 1805–1875. Tommelise. English. II. Title. III. Title: Thumbelina.
PZ8.L854Syl 2010
[398.2]—dc22
[E]
2009004369

Book design by Sara Gillingham.
Typeset in Felina Serif and Bodoni Classic Swashes.
The illustrations in this book were rendered in watercolor and ink.

Manufactured by C&C Offset, Longgang, Shenzhen, China, in November 2009.

10 9 8 7 6 5 4 3 2 1

This product conforms to CPSIA 2008.

Chronicle Books LLC, 680 Second Street, San Francisco, California 94107

www.chroniclekids.com

SYLVIA LONG'S

Thumbelina

chronicle books · san francisco

LONG AGO

in a magical land, there lived a lonely woman who more than anything else in the world wanted to have a child. She had been wishing for a very long time. When her hope began to fade, she went to ask a fairy for advice.

"Please good fairy," the woman said, "I should so very much like to have a child. Can you help me?"

"Of course," replied the fairy. "You are the kindest of women. This barley seed holds the promise of your heart's desire. Plant it and care for it as tenderly as you would your own child and your wish will come true."

The woman hurried home and planted the seed in a flowerpot. She watered it daily, anxiously watching to see what would grow. Soon a sprout appeared and grew into a blossom.

"Such a beautiful flower!" the woman marveled. She bent down to kiss the blossom. As she did, the flower suddenly opened! The woman was amazed to see that in its very center sat a lovely little girl, scarcely as long as the woman's thumb! Delighted, the woman named the girl Thumbelina.

The woman did everything she could to make Thumbelina feel at home. She set out a lovely bowl of water filled with flowers. To Thumbelina it was as big as a lake, and she made herself a flower petal boat, which she rowed about with horse hair oars.

At night, Thumbelina slept in an elegantly polished walnut shell lined with blue violets. A soft rose petal kept her warm. And so Thumbelina lived quite happily . . . until . . . .

. . . one warm night, a large, wet toad hopped through an open
window and leapt upon the table where Thumbelina lay sleeping.

"What a pretty little wife she would make for my son," thought
the toad. She grabbed the walnut shell with Thumbelina in it, and
she jumped back out through the window into the garden.

The old toad carried Thumbelina to the swampy bank of a stream
that flowed along the edge of the garden where she lived with
her son. He was even uglier than his mother and could only cry,
"Croak, croak, croak!" when he saw Thumbelina in her elegant bed.

"Hush or you'll wake her!" whispered his mother. "She might run
away. We will place her on a lily pad out in the stream, where she
cannot escape."

When Thumbelina woke in the morning, she found she was stranded on the lily pad with water on every side as far as she could see! She could not imagine how she had come to this strange place, away from the comfort and love of her home. Thumbelina was frightened and wept miserably.

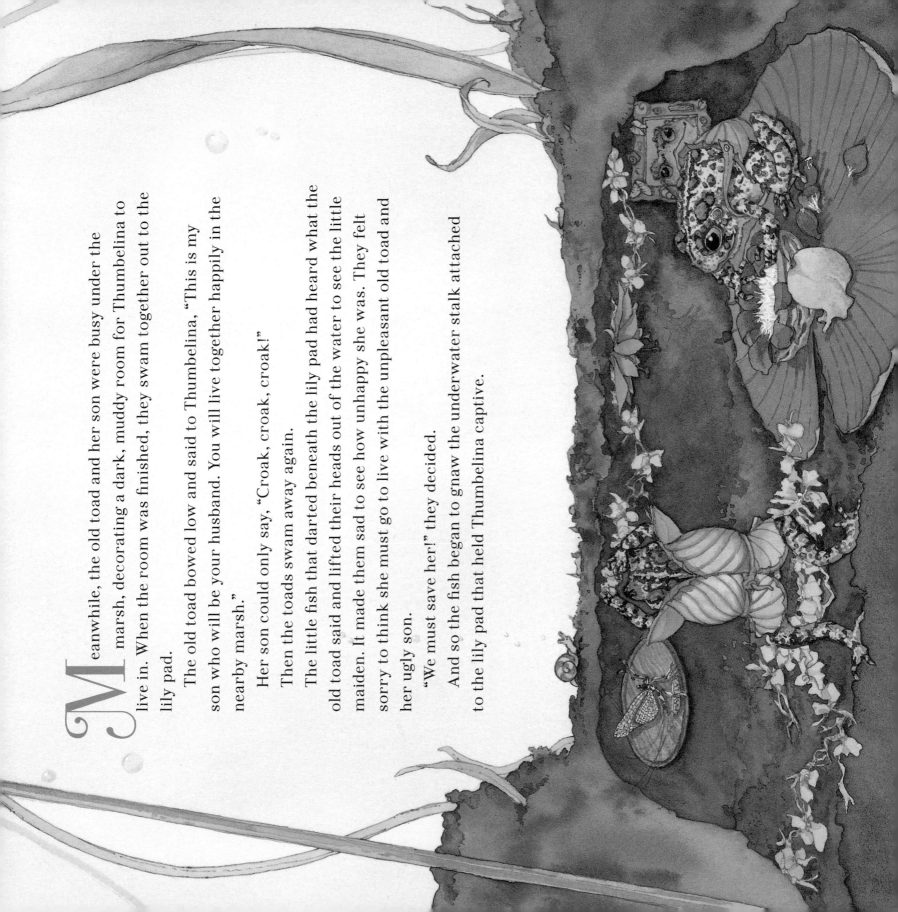

Meanwhile, the old toad and her son were busy under the marsh, decorating a dark, muddy room for Thumbelina to live in. When the room was finished, they swam together out to the lily pad.

The old toad bowed low and said to Thumbelina, "This is my son who will be your husband. You will live together happily in the nearby marsh."

Her son could only say, "Croak, croak, croak!"

Then the toads swam away again.

The little fish that darted beneath the lily pad had heard what the old toad said and lifted their heads out of the water to see the little maiden. It made them sad to see how unhappy she was. They felt sorry to think she must go to live with the unpleasant old toad and her ugly son.

"We must save her!" they decided.

And so the fish began to gnaw the underwater stalk attached to the lily pad that held Thumbelina captive.

Freed from its root, the lily pad drifted quickly down the stream.
Birds who watched from the trees that grew along the banks
were charmed and sang to Thumbelina as she passed by.

A graceful butterfly, wanting to help Thumbelina, lifted the lily pad's long stem from the water and pulled the little craft far from the toad.

But it wasn't just the birds and the butterfly who saw and admired Thumbelina.

A large beetle flying overhead also spied Thumbelina. The moment he saw her, he swooped down and seized her. Thumbelina trembled with fear. What was going to happen to her now?

Holding Thumbelina tightly, the beetle flew with her to a patch of broad leaves near the edge of the stream. He told her she was very pretty, although not in the least like a beetle!

After a while, some other beetles joined them, but they turned
up their antennae disagreeably.

"She has only two legs," said one. "How repulsive!"

"She has no antennae at all," said another, "and her waist is so
slender. Pooh!"

"Oh, she is very ugly!" they all agreed.

Hearing this, the beetle who had grabbed Thumbelina from the
lily pad would have nothing more to do with her and told her she
could go where she liked.

Thumbelina was happy to be free of the beetle, but wept at the
thought that she was so ugly that even the beetles didn't want her
company. She had no way of knowing how lovely she was.

Thumbelina wandered for days before finding her way to a wild forest. She wove herself a bed out of blades of grass and hung it under clover leaves for protection from the rain. She sucked nectar from the flowers for food and drank dew from their leaves every morning.

So passed the summer and the autumn, but then came the cold, harsh winter. The birds who had sung to her so sweetly flew away. The flowers wilted, and the large leaves that had sheltered her for many months shriveled until nothing remained but withered yellow stalks.

hen the snow began to fall, Thumbelina wrapped herself in a
dry leaf, but it cracked and could not keep her warm. So she set
out to find shelter from the cold.

She soon came to a cornfield that had been harvested. Nothing
remained but the dry stubble poking up out of the frozen ground. To
Thumbelina, it was like making her way through a vast wilderness
and she quickly became lost.

At last, Thumbelina came upon the den of a field mouse who lived under the cornfield.

"You poor little creature!" the field mouse exclaimed when she saw Thumbelina. "Come in out of the cold and dine with me." The mouse had a snug kitchen and a whole roomful of corn stored away for the winter. She was happy for the company, so she invited Thumbelina to stay with her until spring.

"You must keep my rooms clean and neat and tell me stories. I love to hear stories!"

Thumbelina did all that the field mouse asked of her and passed the rest of the winter very comfortably.

One day, the field mouse said, "We shall have a visitor soon. My neighbor, the mole, wears a beautiful black velvet coat and his house is twenty times larger than mine. If he were your husband, you would be well provided for indeed."

The mole was wealthy and knew many things, such as how to dig long tunnels through the earth and the best places to find juicy worms and insect grubs. But he did not enjoy sunshine or pretty flowers as Thumbelina did.

When he arrived, Thumbelina was polite and respectful, although she did not feel at all interested in him as a husband.

"Sing for our dear neighbor," prodded the field mouse. And so
Thumbelina sang "Ladybird, Ladybird, Fly Away Home" and many
other songs. The mole was enchanted by her sweet voice.

The mole had dug a tunnel that led from the field mouse's home
to his own. He invited Thumbelina to walk there whenever she liked
but warned her not to be alarmed at the sight of a dead bird that lay
in the passage.

Then the mole took a burning piece of wood from the field
mouse's stove and offered to show them the way. He went before
them through the winding tunnel. The wood glittered in the dark.

As the mole had said, in the middle of the tunnel lay a beautiful
swallow. He must have died from the cold, thought Thumbelina
with a shiver.

The mole brusquely pushed past the bird saying, "He will sing
no more now. How miserable it must be to be born a bird! I am
thankful that none of my children will be birds, for they can do
nothing but whistle and chirp, then die of hunger in the winter."

"Yes, you are wise," the field mouse agreed. "What is the use of
their song?"

Thumbelina said nothing, but when the others had turned their backs, she bent down to stroke the soft feathers that covered the bird's head and kissed his closed eyelids.

"Perhaps you were one who sang to me so sweetly in the summer," she whispered.

That night, Thumbelina could not stop thinking about the swallow. Unable to sleep, she got out of bed and gathered soft down, dried flowers, and strips of corn leaves, which she wove into a blanket as warm as wool.

Nervously, she carried the blanket through the long, dark passageway until she came to the spot where the swallow lay as still as stone. She gently tucked the blanket around the silent swallow.

"Good-bye, lovely bird," she whispered as she bent to give the swallow a final hug farewell.

But when Thumbelina laid her head on the swallow's breast, she heard a faint sound: *thump . . . thump.* It was the swallow's heart, for he was not really dead, only numb from the cold. The warmth of Thumbelina's blanket had restored him.

The rest of the winter, the swallow remained in the tunnel and grew stronger with Thumbelina's tender care. She said nothing about it to the mole or the field mouse, for she knew that they would not approve.

Soon spring came and the sun thawed the frozen earth once more.

One day, the swallow said to Thumbelina, "Because of your tender care, I shall soon regain my strength and be able to fly again." He was very grateful for Thumbelina's kindness and asked if she would go with him.

Thumbelina thought of the green woods and meadows thick with spring flowers that the swallow would visit on his journey, but then she remembered how the field mouse had taken her in when she was cold and hungry.

"I would love to go with you, but I cannot," she answered sadly.

"Farewell then," replied the swallow, "I hope you find the happiness that you deserve." Then he flew out into the brilliant light of day.

As Thumbelina watched him go, tears rose in her eyes. She had become very fond of the dear swallow and knew she would miss his company.

One day the field mouse announced, "What good fortune. My neighbor has asked to marry you! We will make preparations for that special day when you will join the mole to live in his grand home." And so the wedding day was set.

With the help of four expert weavers hired by the field mouse, Thumbelina spent the following weeks gathering flax to spin into linen. They worked day and night, adding bits of wool to keep Thumbelina warm in the mole's chilly home.

Every evening, the mole visited and spoke with longing of the time when summer would be over and they would be married. Thumbelina was not pleased at the thought of spending her life with the tiresome mole, who loved the darkness of his deep hallways. She wished that the summer would never end.

When autumn arrived, Thumbelina's wedding clothes were ready. She sobbed pitifully and said she did not wish to marry the mole and live in darkness beneath the earth.

"Nonsense!" declared the field mouse. "Don't be stubborn or I shall bite you with my sharp teeth! He is a very handsome mole and you are lucky that he wants you. The queen herself does not wear more beautiful velvets. His kitchen and cellars are quite full. You should feel very grateful for this opportunity."

Sadly, Thumbelina counted the days until the mole was to fetch her. Every morning as the sun rose and each evening when it set, Thumbelina slipped to the cornfield so she could watch for a glimpse of sky as the wind parted the tall leaves of corn. She often caught sight of flocks of birds soaring so high above they were but little specks in the brilliant autumn sky.

"Farewell, bright sun! Good-bye sweet friends," she cried.

Early one morning, Thumbelina walked a short distance to where the corn had recently been cut and only dry stubble remained in the fields. Thumbelina wept, as she stood among brilliant red flowers that grew near the field mouse's door.

Suddenly, she heard a familiar sound.

It was the swallow! As soon as he spied
Thumbelina, he swooped down to greet her.
Bitter tears filled her eyes as she told him that
she was soon to marry the mole and live always
beneath the ground, never again to see the
brilliant sun or feel its warmth.

"Will you fly away with me now?" asked the
swallow. "I'll take you far from here, over the
mountains to country where it is always summer.
You saved my life when I lay frozen in that dark
passage and I can't bear to see you so unhappy.
Please come with me, dear little Thumbelina."

Thumbelina climbed onto the swallow's back and held on tightly as the bird rose high into the air. The swallow flew over forest and sea, above the tallest mountain peaks, forever covered with snow. Thumbelina tucked herself under the swallow's feathers to keep warm in the frigid air, but she kept her head uncovered as they soared so she could see the beautiful lands that passed beneath them.

At last they reached a meadow filled with wildflowers. The sun shone brightly on trees heavy with lemons and oranges. Long vines of purple, green, and white grapes climbed dazzling marble pillars and the air was fragrant with honeysuckle and gardenias.

They flew by an ancient palace. High on the walls were many swallows' nests. One of these was the home of Thumbelina's friend.

"You are welcome to stay with me," he said, "but I don't think you would be happy living so high above the ground."

The swallow landed in a small meadow near three broken pieces of a marble pillar.

"Here you will be comfortable and have all you've wished for," said the swallow. Then he placed her on the sturdy leaf of a large white flower.

How surprised Thumbelina was to see in the flower's center a man scarcely larger than herself! He had a golden crown upon his head and delicate wings at his shoulders.

When he saw Thumbelina, he was delighted. Her beauty and kindness glowed from within and she looked so enchanting to him that he fell immediately in love with her.

The prince placed his golden crown upon her head and asked if she would be his wife and queen of his fairy kingdom.

Thumbelina's heart filled with joy. She knew
that he would be a much better husband than
the horrible toad who would only say, "Croak,
croak, croak," the disagreeable beetle, or the
gloomy mole.